MOMMY
ALWAYS COMES BACK

Written by
Karen Landon Moore

Illustrated by
Clarice Diamantino

This book is dedicated to my mother,
Virginia Bond Landon.
We dreamed about writing a
children's book together one day.
It never actually happened for us,
but she is here in the pages of this one.

Copyright ©2026 Karen Landon Moore
Written by Karen Landon Moore
Illustrated by Clarice Diamantino

Photo of Karen Landon Moore by Alex Paul Photography
Photo of Clarice Diamantino by Bia Braz

Published by Miriam Laundry Publishing Company
miriamlaundry.com

HC ISBN 978-1-77944-609-1
PB ISBN 978-1-77944-608-4
e-Book ISBN 978-1-77944-607-7

FIRST EDITION

About the Author

Karen Moore was an elementary and special education teacher, but her greatest joy was raising her four children. Now, as a grandparent, she gets to watch her grandchildren navigate their way through the milestones in their lives. This story was inspired by the single tear rolling down her grandson's cheek on his first day of preschool.

She hopes that this book will help to put other children's worries to rest as they go off to their first day of school, too!

You can learn more about Karen at:

f karen.landonmoore   **◎** @karenlandonmoore

About the Illustrator

Clarice Diamantino is a Brazilian illustrator based in Lisbon, where she lives with her husband and their adorable dog, Caju. Clarice's love of illustration began in childhood, watching her uncle transform blank pages into her beloved characters. This early fascination led her to pursue a degree in Graphic Design and find her passion. Telling cute visual stories that resonate with global audiences has been her drive and everyday joy ever since.

Sam picked out a brand-new dinosaur lunch box and dinosaur backpack for this special day—his first day of preschool!

Mommy and Daddy told Sam he would have fun there.

"I want to go, too," cried his little brother, Rory.

"You have to get big like me first," said Sam.

"I'm going to wear my light-up
shoes today," said Sam.
He looked everywhere for them.

"Rory!" he yelled. "Those don't fit you!"

He took the shoes
from his brother and
grabbed his backpack.

"Come on," he said.
"We can't be late."

7

WELCOME TO PRESCH[OOL]

"Look, Sam! Your classroom is blue—
your favorite color!" said Mommy.

8

"Welcome, Sam," said a nice lady. "I'm Miss Judy. We're going to have so much fun today!"

Miss Judy kind of smelled like strawberries.

9

The room was filled with boys and girls, and toys and books.

JOEY SAM ELLY

Sam looked at his brother. "I wish you could stay and play with me, Rory," he said.

Sam's tummy started to feel funny. He looked
up at Mommy and squeezed her hand tight.

"It's okay, Sam," she said. "Remember what I told you?"

"Yes," said Sam. "Mommy always comes back."

"That's right," she replied. She gave him a kiss.
"I will see you soon."

Sam waved at Mommy and Rory until
he couldn't see them anymore.

KARLA JOEY SAM ELLY

The little girl sitting next to Sam looked scared, too. Sam wanted to tell her that mommies always come back, but the teacher called his name.

14

It was his turn to paint—with his FINGERS!

He stuck his fingers in the blue paint. After all, blue was his favorite color. It felt cold and wet, and smooth and squishy. It oozed right up between all his fingers! Before he knew it, his whole hand was covered in blue paint.

15

Sam pressed his hand on the paper. It looked like a dinosaur footprint. He made red footprints, yellow footprints, and green footprints. He knew Mommy and Daddy were really going to love his new painting.

The toys at school were different than the ones Sam had at home. He saw an area filled with blocks. He was good at building things, so he went over to explore.

A little girl already sitting there said, "Hi. My name is Sophie. You have to build a castle." She looked mad.

"Why?" he asked.

"I love castles best," she said. "But look—mine keeps falling down."

18

Sam had an idea.

"I'll help you build the tallest castle you ever saw," he said.
"And then you can help me build a bridge for it."

The castle got taller and taller, and Sophie got happier and happier.

"Thank you, Sam," she said.
She had a big smile on her face.

Sam was glad he could help.

KARLA　　JOEY　　SAM　　ELLY

When Miss Judy called, "Snack Time!" Sam ran to get his dinosaur lunch box. He bumped right into another boy.

"Hi, I'm Joey," said the boy.

"Look," said Sam. "We have the same lunch box!"

21

While Sam and Joey ate their snacks together, they named all the dinosaurs on their lunch boxes.

"T-Rex is my favorite," said Joey.

"Mine too," said Sam.

Joey roared loudly at Sam and Sam roared right back.

ROAR!

ROAR!

"Boys," said Miss Judy. "Not so loud, please."

Miss Judy started passing out rest-time mats.
Sam *was* getting pretty tired.

"May I have the blue one?" asked Sam.

"Of course!" said Miss Judy.

24

Sam lay on the mat thinking about Mommy and Rory. He wondered what they were doing right now.

As his eyes started to close, he remembered that Mommy always comes back. He drifted off to sleep.

Later, Sam and Joey sat next to each other for story time.

"Did everyone have a fun day today?" asked Miss Judy.

"Yes!" the class called out together. Even the little girl who had looked scared this morning looked happy now.

"I can't wait to come back!" hollered Joey.

KARLA JOEY SAM ELLY

Sam put his backpack on
and got ready to go home.

Miss Judy led them all out into a crowded hall full of big people with big shoes, and little people with little shoes. Sam felt very small. He reached for Miss Judy's hand.

Once they were outside, Sam looked around.
Where's Mommy? What if she forgot to come back?

There she was!

Sam ran over and gave
his mommy a giant hug.
He then hugged Rory, too.

A tear rolled down Sam's cheek.
It was a very, very happy tear.

Now he knew it was really true...

Mommy always comes back!

www.ingramcontent.com/pod-product-compliance
Lightning Source LLC
Chambersburg PA
CBHW042147240326

41723CB00014B/619